TANZANIA

JAHA AND JAMIL

Jaha and Jamil went down the hill
To fetch a pail of water.
They met Atu and Siwatu
And Asha with her daughter.

CHICORY, PICKORY, POCK

Chicory, Pickory, Pock,
Lizard ran up the rock.
Snake showed its fang,
Down Lizard sprang.
Chicory, Pickory, Pock.

PANGOLIN

Pangolin, pangolin,
unfurl for me,
Curled in a branch at
the top of our tree.
With scales in
layers, you hang in
your home,
Looking to all like a
giant pine cone.

JAHA AND JAMIL WENT DOWN THE HILL

AN AFRICAN MOTHER GOOSE

by VIRGINIA KROLL

illustrated by KATHERINE ROUNDTREE

 Charlesbridge

For Carole Brocious, poet at heart – V.K.
For my friends at the Cincinnati Public Library – K.R.

Author's Note: The verses in this book are those that Mother Goose might have written, had she visited Africa. The rhymes, with which many children are familiar, contain different lyrics that teach about a few of the wonderful, colorful, diverse aspects of African life, both modern and traditional.

The poems in JAHA AND JAMIL WENT DOWN THE HILL correspond to the following Mother Goose rhymes:

Jack and Jill
Hickory Dickory Dock
Curly Locks
Mary Had a Little Lamb
Where, Oh Where?
Ride a Cock Horse to
    Banbury Cross
Hark, Hark
Diddle Diddle Dumpling
Pease Porridge Hot
Peter, Peter
Little Miss Muffet
Two Little Dicky Birds
London Bridge
Polly Put the Kettle On
To Market
E Was the Escalator
Sing a Song of Sixpence
One, Two, Three, Four, Five
Tom, Tom the Piper's Son
Little Bo Peep
Old Woman on the Hill
Hey Diddle Diddle
Pat-a-Cake
Pussycat, Pussycat

Little Tommy Tucker
Ring Around the Rosy
Little Tommy Tiddlemouse
Fee-Fi-Fo-Fum
Rock-a-Bye Baby
Three Men in a Tub
A Tisket, A Tasket
Dapple Gray
Little Boy Blue
Handy Pandy
Mary, Mary
The Queen of Hearts
My Sister and I
Bat, Bat
Old Woman in a Shoe
Pop Goes the Weasel
Yankee Doodle
Here We Go 'Round the
    Mulberry Bush
Pit-Pat, Well-a-Day!
How Many Miles to Babylon?
Bat, Bat
One, Two
Row, Row, Row Your Boat
One for the Money

Text and illustrations Copyright © 1995 by Charlesbridge Publishing
All rights reserved, including the right of reproduction in whole or in part in any form.

Published by Charlesbridge Publishing
85 Main Street, Watertown, MA 02472 · (617) 926-0329
www.charlesbridge.com

Library of Congress Cataloging-in-Publication Data
Kroll, Virginia L.
    Jaha and Jamil went down the hill: an African Mother Goose / by Virginia Kroll; illustrated by Katherine Roundtree.
        p.   cm.
    ISBN 0-88106-865-9 (softcover)
    ISBN 0-88106-866-7 (reinforced for library use)
    I. Mother Goose–Parodies, imitations, etc. 2. Children's poetry, American.
3. Africa–Juvenile poetry. [I. Nursery rhymes– Adaptations. 2. American poetry.
3. Africa–Poetry.] I. Roundtree, Katherine, ill. II. Title.
PS3561.R58313 1994
811'.54–dc20
                                                    93-30634
                                                       CIP
                                                       AC

Printed in the United States of America
(sc) 10 9 8 7 6 5 4
(hc) 10 9 8 7 6 5 4 3

RUZIBA HAD A SMOKY BIRD

Ruziba had a smoky bird
With tail feathers red.
It perched upon his shoulder,
It sat upon his head.

It imitated every beast
From elephant to goat
And scared him like a lion
When it roared deep in its
throat.

WHERE, OH WHERE?

Where, oh where
has my colobus gone?
Where, oh where
can he be?
With his ears so short and his tail so long,
Oh where, oh where can he be?

BURUNDI

DANCE OF THE TUTSI

Go past the trees of the jungle, please,
To see Tutsi dancers jump in the breeze.
They wear leopard skins and leap so high,
Twirling and whirling like birds in the sky.

Look at the Tutsi so big and so tall
Who dance out their stories for one and for all.
Rings around ankles, feathers in hair,
Graceful as antelopes, soaring through air.

HARK, HARK! WILD DOGS DO BARK

Hark . . . Hark!
Wild dogs do bark.
Gazelles are coming down,
Some with freckles
And some with speckles
And most in coats of brown.

BALAFON

Tap, tap, trill, trill balafon,
Played at the market, played on the lawn,
Making merry music from dusk till dawn,
Tap, tap, trill, trill balafon.

SENEGAL

KALAHARI DAYS HOT

Kalahari days hot,
Kalahari days cold,
Baby in a kaross cape
Nine days old.
Block out the desert heat,
Keep out the desert cold,
Baby in a kaross cape
Nine days old.

TALEH, TALEH

Taleh, Taleh needed water
For her thirsty little daughter,
Put it in an ostrich shell
And there she kept it very well.

DANJUMA

Danjuma sat down
On the soft ground
To eat his curds and whey.
Along came a flock
That gave him a shock
And frightened Danjuma away.

TWO BIRDS

Two thick-billed birds
Sitting in a wall,
One named Cuckoo,
The other named Coucal.
Fly away, Cuckoo!
Fly away, Coucal!
Come back, Cuckoo!
Come back, Coucal!

CANOPIES ARE FALLING DOWN

Canopies are falling down,
Falling down, falling down.
Canopies are falling down,
Sad rain forest!

Plant new trees and build them up,
Build them up, build them up.
Plant new trees and build them up,
Glad rain forest!!!

MAMA, PUT YOUR HEADCLOTH ON

Mama, put your headcloth on,
Mama, put your headcloth on,
Mama, put your headcloth on,
Tied 'round your head.

Mama, take it off again,
Mama, take it off again,
Mama, take it off again.
It's time for bed.

TO MARKET

To market, to market
To buy dates and plums.
Home again, home
To the beating of drums!

GHANA

ALPHABET RHYME

A is the aardvark looking for his lunch.

B is the baboon with bugs in a bunch.

C is the crocodile, cruising through reeds.

D is the dove on a diet of seeds.

E is the elephant heading the herd.

F is the feathery finfoot bird.

G is the guenon with long, curving tail.

H is hyena, hot on the trail.

I is impala, imagine their flight!

J is the jackal, a-jabber at night.

K is the kite bird aloft in the air.

L is the lioness guarding her lair.

M is the manioc in a wood dish.

N is the new net they use to catch fish.

O is the ostrich with eyesight so keen.

P is the pangolin hiding, unseen.

Q is queléas in quarrelsome flocks.

R is the rhino reclining near rocks.

S is the shrew,
darting fast as it could.
T is the termite that
tastes the dead wood.
U is uranium up from
the mine.
V is the viper snake
coiled like a vine.
W is wildebeest
galloping free.

X is the xylophone's sweet melody.
Y is the yam growing ready to eat.
Z is the zebra with stripes head to feet.

ZIMBABWE

SING A SONG OF BIRD CALLS

Sing a song of bird calls
From the eastern sky
Millions, billions, trillions,
Winging wildly by,
Looking like a black cloud
Right before a storm,
Zillions of queléa birds
Gathered in a swarm!

COUNTING FISH

One, two, three, four, five —
I caught a Nile perch alive!
Six, seven, eight, nine, ten —
We had ten fish, and then again!

DRISS, DRISS, THE FARMER'S SON

Driss, Driss, the farmer's son
Bought a goat and away did run.
The goat did bleat; its milk was sweet,
And Driss went skipping down the street.

LITTLE AHMED HAS LOST HIS GOATS

Little Ahmed has lost his goats
And rushes right out to find them.
Don't leave them alone! They must come home,
For Dog is right behind them!

MOROCCO

SOUTH AFRICA

AARDVARK ON THE HILL

There was an old aardvark
Who lived in a hill,
And if he's not gone,
He lives there still.

IN THE AFRICAN AIR

Hey, diddle diddle, Cricket did fiddle
While
Firefly
mimicked
the moon.
Wildebeest rumbled
While Wild Dog grumbled,
And Lion chased after
Baboon.

BEND A WIRE

Bend a wire, bend a wire,
Coppersmith man.
Make me a bracelet
Fast as you can.
Swerve it and curve it
And add a nice charm,
So Mama will wear it
Each day on her arm.

LITTLE CHILD

Little child, little child,
Where are you from?
Far off in Africa, under the sun.
Little child, little child,
What do you eat?
Cassava and fishes, oh what a treat!

LITTLE THAKO THAMBO

Little Thako Thambo
Sings for his supper.
What shall we give him?
Sweet goat's milk butter!

RING AROUND THE SAND DUNE

Ring around the sand dune,
Chanting an oasis tune.
Water, water,
We drink it down!

TUAREG MEN

Tuareg men in clothes of blue
Talk and trade and business do,
Uncovering their faces
At the oasis.

ALGERIA

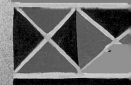

FEE, FI, FO, FOO

Fee, fi, fo, foo.
I smell the juice of vegetable stew.
With a scarf around my head,
I'll grind the manioc to make our bread.

ROCK-A-BYE BABY

Rock-a-bye baby in Mama's shawl,
Snuggled up tightly, round as a ball.
When Mama bends,
You'll dip and you'll sway
Like leaves in a soft breeze
All through the day.

NICHES AND NOOK

Niches and nook,
Three men in a souk.
Who do you think they may be?
The carver, the baker,
The cotton cloth maker.
Buy their fine wares, all three.

A TISKET, A TASKET

A tisket, a tasket,
A red and yellow basket.
I bought a fish for the stew
And going home, I lost it.
I lost it, I lost it.
And going home I lost it.
I bought a fish for the stew
And going home, I lost it.

KENYA

I HAD A LITTLE BABY

I had a little baby
And it was made of clay.
I'd wrap it in a scrap of cloth
And go outside to play.

LITTLE MAASAI

Little Maasai,
Come blow your horn.
Your cattle are hungry,
A new calf is born.
Where is the boy
Who looks after the herd?
He's under the acacia tree
Chasing a bird.

BOLD KHALFANI

Bold Khalfani, brave Khalfani
Loves to eat sweet amber honey,
Lights a torch and scales the trees
To reach into a hive of bees!

TALL NALONGO

Tall Nalongo with your long hoe,
How does your garden grow?
With millet grains and green plantains
And tasty yams all in a row.

MOZAMBIQUE

MAMA JAKES

Mama Jakes, she made some cakes out of new-ground millet. She fattened them, Then flattened them, And cooked them on her skillet.

KOLA AND TEA

Nomsa, my sister, started to pout, And what do you think it was all about? She wanted kola and I wanted tea, And that was the reason we couldn't agree.

MASK, MASK

Mask, mask, what a task
To carve an expression dread,
Scaring, delighting,
Bewaring, exciting,
With feathers on its head.

THERE WAS AN OLD WOMAN

There was an old woman
Who lived by the Nile.
She grew figs and beans
In a very grand style.
She worked night and day
To pull out the weeds,
To water her garden
And plant flower seeds.

POKE GOES THE WEEVIL

All around the cotton rows
And through her fields so level.
That's the way the cotton boll grows.
Poke goes the weevil!

OLD CHAMELEON

Old chameleon came to town,
Passing by a lemur.
He curled his tail and fell asleep
Because he was a dreamer.

Old chameleon do wake up,
Old chameleon funny,
Spread your toes to run and leap
And play while it is sunny.

THE EBONY TREE

Here we go round the ebony tree,
The ebony tree, the ebony tree.
Here we go round the ebony tree
On a hot and humid morning.

NAMIBIA

PIT-PAT, WELL-A-DAY!

Pit-Pat, well-a-day!
Little Momar went to play.
Where can little Momar be?
With his friends in the big city.

HOW MANY MILES?

How many miles to Tunisia?
Three score miles and ten.
Can I get there by firefly light?
Yes, and back again.
If your heels are
nimble and light,
You may get there
by firefly light.

RIP, RAP

Rip, rap, draw the flap,
Sit by the fire and listen.
Grandma's stories and Grandpa's glories
Will make your eyelights glisten.

ONE, TWO, EAT FISH STEW

One, two, eat fish stew.
Three, four, watch rains pour.
Five, six, dry the sticks.
Seven, eight, munch a date.
Nine, ten, begin again.

SPREAD, SPREAD, SPREAD YOUR NET

Spread, spread, spread your net
Gently in the sea,
Gathering, gathering, gathering, gathering
Fish for you and me.

ALL AROUND AFRICA

One for the Zulu   (ZOO loo)

Two for the San   (san)

Three for the Samburu   (sam BOO roo)

Four for the Dan   (dan)

Five for the Ashanti   (uh SHAN tee)

Six for the Ewe   (EH vay)

Seven for the Fulani   (foo LAH nee)

Eight for the Uge   (OO gay)

Nine for the Yoruba   (your OO bah)

Ten for the Vai   (vie)

Eleven for the Dinka   (DING ka)

Twelve for Maasai   (mah SIGH)

MOROCCO

TUNISIA

ALGERIA

LIBYA

EGYPT

WESTERN
SAHARA

MAURITANIA

MALI

NIGER

CHAD

SUDAN

DJIBOUTI

SENEGAL

GAMBIA

BURKINA
FASO

Lake Chad

GUINEA
BISSAU

GUINEA

NIGERIA

ETHIOPIA

SIERRA
LEONE

IVORY
COAST

GHANA

CENTRAL
AFRICAN REPUBLIC

SOMALIA

LIBERIA

BENIN
TOGO

CAMEROON

UGANDA

KENYA

GABON

CONGO

ZAIRE

RWANDA

Lake
Victoria

BURUNDI

TANZANIA

ANGOLA

ZAMBIA

MALAWI

NAMIBIA

ZIMBABWE

MOZAMBIQUE

MADAGASCAR

BOTSWANA

SWAZILAND

SOUTH
AFRICA

LESOTHO